Joins the Team

Story by
Danny Ramadan

Art by
Anna Bron

toronto · berkeley

© 2024 Danny Ramadan (text)
© 2024 Anna Bron (illustrations)

Cover art by Anna Bron, designed by Sam Tse
Interior design by Sam Tse
Cover and interior based on the series design by Paul Covello

Edited by Claire Caldwell
Copy edited by Kateri Couture-Latour
Proofread by Eleanor Gasparik

Annick Press Ltd.
All rights reserved. No part of this work covered by the copyrights hereon may be reproduced or used in any form or by any means—graphic, electronic, or mechanical—without the prior written permission of the publisher.

We acknowledge the support of the Canada Council for the Arts and the Ontario Arts Council, and the participation of the Government of Canada/ la participation du gouvernement du Canada for our publishing activities.

ONTARIO ARTS COUNCIL
CONSEIL DES ARTS DE L'ONTARIO
an Ontario government agency
un organisme du gouvernement de l'Ontario

Library and Archives Canada Cataloguing in Publication

Title: Salma joins the team / story by Danny Ramadan ; art by Anna Bron.
Names: Ramadan, Ahmad Danny, author. | Bron, Anna, 1989- illustrator.
Identifiers: Canadiana (print) 20230509959 | Canadiana (ebook) 20230509967 | ISBN 9781773218281 (hardcover) | ISBN 9781773218298 (softcover) | ISBN 9781773218304 (EPUB) | ISBN 9781773218311 (PDF)
Classification: LCC PS8635.A4613 S22 2024 | DDC jC813/.6—dc23

Published in the U.S.A. by Annick Press (U.S.) Ltd.
Distributed in Canada by University of Toronto Press.
Distributed in the U.S.A. by Publishers Group West.

Printed in Canada

annickpress.com
dannyramadan.com
annabron.com

Also available as an e-book. Please visit annickpress.com/ebooks for more details.

To my team: Matthew, Cee, Samantha, and Bradley.
—D.R.

To Andrew, thanks for being my teammate all these years.
—A.B.

Table of Contents

Chapter 1	1
Chapter 2	12
Chapter 3	20
Chapter 4	31
Chapter 5	41
Chapter 6	53
Chapter 7	61
Chapter 8	70
Chapter 9	78
Chapter 10	88

Chapter 1

Salma has a big question to ask, but she doesn't know where to start. She hovers in her bedroom doorway, watching Mama breastfeed her new baby sister, Nora, in the living room.

"Hi, Salma. Do you need anything?" Mama asks while the baby coos.

"Nope. Nothing," Salma says, losing her nerve.

"Well, it feels like there is something," Mama says

playfully. She pats the couch beside her. "Come sit with us."

Salma pauses, then crosses over to sit by Mama's side. She bounces her legs on the couch, still not sure how to bring this up with her mother. Mama tightens the shawl around Nora, then looks Salma in the eye.

"Salma," Mama says, "what do you want?"

It's now or never, Salma thinks. "Mama, you know how much I love Yusra Mardini, right?"

Mama nods. "Of course." Over the past few months, Mama has helped Salma redecorate her room: there are pictures of Mardini standing by the Olympic torch, a poster of her bundled up in a towel after winning a qualifying swimming race, and a little replica of an Olympic gold medal hanging on the wall.

"Well, today I shared a video of her with my class."

Salma pictures it: the swimmer standing proudly at the edge of the pool. She doesn't look nervous. Like Salma, she has light tanned skin with some dimples and birthmarks. A wisp of hair—chestnut brown, just like Salma's—escapes her swimming cap. Her eyes are the color of honey, Salma knows, even though Yusra is wearing goggles.

"All my friends loved Yusra," Salma insists.

She remembers her friend Riya turning to her in excitement when the video finished. "Yusra is so cool. She went through so much, but now she's thriving!"

"It's very common for immigrants and refugees to be successful when given the chance," Ms. Singh said.

"Yusra is my new favorite Olympian," Ayman added. "I don't know any other Olympians, but she is my favorite for sure."

Even though she'd seen the video many times, Salma's eyes had been glued to the big screen, watching her hero doing the butterfly—breaking the surface of the water, and splashing it in an arc over her head, pushing herself forward with purpose.

"I wish I could swim like Yusra," Salma told her classmates.

And that's when Ms. Singh had shared the most amazing thing ever. The thing Salma needs to ask Mama about now.

"Maybe you can be like Yusra!" Ms. Singh had said. "There's a swimming club here at school!"

Salma doesn't know how to swim and no one in her family has ever been to a swimming pool. But Ms. Singh had explained that she could learn to swim if she joined the club. If she worked hard, she could even try out for the school swim team. And if she made it onto the team, she'd get to race against other schools!

All she needs is her parents' permission.

Salma leans into Mama's side and lets images of her possible future fill her head. She, too, could dive elegantly into the swimming pool. She could push the water with her arms and legs until she floated on its surface like a butterfly. She could win all the Olympic medals in the world and carry them around her neck proudly.

"That's nice, Salma." Mama's voice breaks into her thoughts. "It's always wonderful to share your interests with friends. But was there something else you wanted to ask me?"

Salma takes a deep breath. She is scared to ask her question. What if Mama says no? But there's only one way to find out.

"Mama, I want to join the school swim club," she says in a rush. She shares what Ms. Singh told her. Mama leans back and rocks the baby softly. Then she gets up and puts Nora in her crib.

"Mama? Why aren't you answering?" Salma asks. "Are you afraid I will drown?"

"Oh, don't say that! Of course not," Mama says, busying herself with the dishes. "You are a strong girl, and I am sure the school has many lifeguards."

"Then what is it, Mama?" Salma pulls at Mama's robe. Mama sighs. She turns off the tap and bends down to Salma's eye level.

"Honestly, Salma, the problem is that our religion and traditions say that girls cannot wear revealing outfits in public," Mama says. "That includes the swimsuit you will have to wear if you join this sport."

Wait, what? Salma's never thought about that before. She wears long sleeves more often than most of the other girls at school, and there is a section of her closet for the clothes she can wear to the mosque. But she's never really thought about why . . . or that wearing a swimsuit would be a problem. "I don't understand. Yusra wears a swimsuit all the time."

"There are many different cultures, religions, and traditions in Syria. We come from a more traditional background than Yusra." Mama reminds Salma of the other Syrian women they meet when they go to the mosque. They wear long sleeves, and long skirts, too. And they all wear the hijab around their heads like Mama. "For Syrians like our family and the people who go to our mosque, wearing a swimsuit could be seen as disrespectful."

Salma doesn't want to be disrespectful. She loves going to the mosque—it's the only time she meets other Syrian girls, as none of them go to her school. But she wants to be like Yusra Mardini, who is also a Syrian girl, even if she is from a different background. It's not like Salma would wear her swimsuit to the mosque!

"Please just think about it, Mama." Salma channels Yusra's determination. "I really want to be part of this swim team. It means the whole world to me, Mama."

Mama's face softens. She pulls Salma in for a hug and kisses her on the forehead. "I will think about it, Salma," Mama says. "I will discuss it with Baba and let you know what we decide."

Salma nods. She will do whatever her parents think is best, but she hopes they will make the right decision and let her swim.

Chapter 2

"Salma, you're going to be late for school!"

Mama's voice is soft and singsong-like. Salma opens her eyes to the bright fall light coming through her window. She flips over and buries her face in her soft pillow. She was having the most wonderful dream. Ice cream mountains and unicorn ponies and all the good cotton candy clouds she could ever ask for. She would much rather go back to her dreamland.

"Salma!"

With sleep still in her eyes, Salma turns over and sighs. It's unfair that she has to wake up early for school! She wishes everyone would just go back

to bed so she could stay in hers. This soft, warm, cozy bed with her fluffy pink pillow . . .

Salma's eyes land on her poster of Yusra. It has been almost a week since she asked her mama for permission to join the swimming club, and she hasn't gotten an answer yet. Maybe today is the day.

"Okay!" Salma finally jumps out of bed.

"We have raised the laziest girl in the world," Baba teases when he sees her exiting her bedroom. He sips his cup of Turkish coffee while cradling little Nora in his other arm. Mama prepares their lunch boxes in the kitchen.

"I am not lazy!" Salma says. "I'm just selective about where I spend my energy."

"Spend your energy on getting ready for school, then," Mama says.

Salma huffs in annoyance and walks back into her room. She stuffs her schoolbooks in her bag, quickly makes her bed, then lays out her clothes before she grabs her towel and heads toward the shower.

"Hey, before you do that, come over here for a second," Baba says. Salma turns on her heel and stomps toward the kitchen. She stands, arms crossed, towel on her shoulder, and waits for her baba to speak. Baba puts down his cup of coffee, then ruffles her unruly hair.

"Wow, you really don't like mornings," Baba says.

"I like them a lot, actually," Salma says. "I just wish they happened in the afternoon."

Mama and Baba burst out laughing. After a second, Salma joins them, and the baby giggles, too. *Mornings are not that bad*, Salma thinks. She gets to spend time with her three favorite people in the world.

"Well, maybe this will make your morning better." Baba picks up a gym bag that Salma hadn't noticed before and hands it to her. It's heavier than she expects.

"What is this?" Salma is puzzled.

"It's a surprise," Mama says. "Open it up!"

Salma unzips the bag and digs her arm into it up to the elbow. She feels something round and plastic and pulls it out.

"Swimming goggles!" Salma's sleepiness evaporates on the spot. She shrieks in excitement. "What? What does this mean?"

"Keep digging, Salma," Baba says with a joyful smile.

Salma pulls out a beautiful swimming cap with little jasmine flowers printed on it, a yellow snorkel, and a small kickboard she can float on while training.

There is a white cotton towel, and a water bottle, too. She touches something smooth and stretchy and pulls it out. It's a swimsuit: black, with sporty white trim.

"This is the best surprise ever!" Salma jumps and hugs her baba around the neck. All of her new swimming gear falls to the ground. "Thank you so much."

"Well, your mama and I spoke, and we decided that you should do whatever brings you joy," Baba says.

Mama walks over. Salma gives her a hug, and Mama kisses Salma's forehead. "Whatever makes you happy, Salma." Mama hands Salma a piece of paper with a signature at the bottom. "Here is your permission slip."

Salma feels like the luckiest girl alive. The warmth gathering in her chest travels up to her face. "Thank you so much, Mama and Baba. You are the best parents in the world."

Who's Your Hero?

Salma decided to become a swimmer because of her hero, Yusra Mardini. Many kids—and even adults—have their own heroes, too. Your hero can be anybody: a celebrity, a fictional character, or someone you know! But most heroes have a few things in common:

Baba brings Salma in for a closer hug, and Mama joins them. They hold on to one another for a moment.

"Now, go get ready for school." Mama rolls up her sleeves, returning to the kitchen.

"See? Mornings don't have to be such a bad thing," Baba adds.

Salma gathers her new swimming gear and takes it toward her bedroom. "I am not saying I'm changing my views on mornings, but I will consider today as a better example."

She hears her parents laugh again as she looks up at her posters of Yusra Mardini. She sees the swimmer's wide smile and the joy of winning on her face. "I will make you proud," Salma promises. "I will win every race. But first, I have to learn how to swim!"

Chapter 3

In the girls' changeroom, Salma takes a deep breath, then turns around to face the mirror.

Her reflection looks terrified. Her eyes are wide, her lips are tight, and her cheeks are white like paper. Maybe she is not ready for this. Maybe she will drown today. The pool's water is warm, but not warm enough. She will freeze, and all her muscles will go numb, and then she will drown.

Her swimsuit is not helping. Salma has never been out in public in such a small outfit, even in the summer. Her arms are exposed. Her legs are cold. She tugs the neckline up. It's hard to breathe.

"Salma?" Riya calls from the door to the pool. "The coach sent me to check on you. Where are you?" Though Riya is not in the swimming club, she came to support Salma for her first lesson.

Salma quickly wraps herself in her towel. "I'm here." Her voice shakes.

"What's wrong, Salma?" Riya approaches and takes her hand. "The training started five minutes ago."

"I'm just afraid." Salma leans on her friend.

"Maa says that what matters is that we try our best," Riya says. She tightens her hand on Salma's. "You can do that for sure."

Salma nods, but she is not sure she wants to do this anymore. She really wants to be a swimmer. This swimsuit doesn't feel good on her, but Salma knows she has to wear it to get in the water.

"C'mon, Salma," Riya insists. "You got this."

Salma hesitates for a second, then walks toward the pool with her best friend.

The moment she steps through the changeroom door, she hears the shouts of everyone in the water. Mr. Heatherington, the Physical Education teacher, stands in his red tracksuit with a whistle in his mouth. He is the tallest teacher in the whole school, and he always looks like he just finished a run.

"I will be right here," Riya whispers. Salma squeezes her hand one last time, then watches her head back to the bleachers on one side of the pool.

"Salma! Come here," Mr. Heatherington calls. Salma hurries toward him, careful not to slip in the puddles everywhere. She notices Ayman swimming laps. On a tall chair, an older boy in shorts and a red jacket keeps his eyes on everyone in case of an emergency.

"Hello, Mr. Heatherington," Salma says quietly. She has to crane her neck more than usual to see his face.

"Salma? Where is your kickboard?" the PE teacher asks. Salma realizes she forgot it in the changeroom. She feels tears gathering in her eyes. This is not going well at all.

"I am glad that you joined us, Salma," Mr. Heatherington says. "But we need to set some ground rules here: never be late to training, always come prepared, and do your best every single time."

Salma nods. She sniffs in her tears. This is

her dream. She is better than this, and she will do everything she needs to do.

"Here, use this kickboard for now," Mr. Heatherington says. "We are going to start with some flutter kicking, to see where we are."

For the next forty minutes, Salma stays in the shallow end of the pool, kicking her feet and learning how to float. Mr. H. is strict. He speaks in short sentences and insists on good form. Somehow, that makes Salma feel better. Mr. H. knows exactly what he is doing.

"Salma, you may try out the deep end now with your kickboard," Mr. H. says. "We will all keep an eye on you."

Salma nods. She holds on to the board, and walks, water dripping from her feet, to the deeper end of

the pool. Her heart beats faster, but she takes a deep breath and tightens her fingers on the foam edge of the board. She stands by the pool, looking at all her classmates leaning on their boards and paddling away with their feet splashing water everywhere. She remembers Yusra standing at the edge of an Olympic pool, diving elegantly into the water. She will be that strong; she will be as elegant as her idol. Salma pulls the goggles over her eyes, holds the board to her chest with both arms, and jumps right in.

Salma sinks feet first into the pool. She squeezes the board and keeps her cheeks full of air like balloons. The sound of her friends' shouting dims. She firmly shuts her eyes, too. The water is colder in the deep end, but slowly it turns refreshing. She points her toes and they touch the bottom of the pool. She opens her eyes and sees everyone splashing above her, playful and happy. The water murmurs to her softly. Somehow, her anxiety evaporates, and she is now at peace.

Salma feels a smile forming on her face underwater.

The kickboard pulls Salma up, and she emerges from the water. She takes a deep breath, then laughs in joy. She loves the water so much. She moves her feet and feels the water flowing over her skin, bubbles floating everywhere. She kicks, suddenly moving fast like a little dolphin. She rests her elbows on the kickboard, kicking even faster. She laughs loudly, then lifts one arm to wave at Riya.

That makes Salma lose her balance.

She slips off of the board and sinks to the bottom of the pool.

Salma's arms and legs spread out like a starfish.

She can see the surface, where her kickboard floats by itself, and her chest tightens. Salma just learned how to float, but panic fills her head. What is she supposed to do? Did anyone notice her slip? Will they come to help her?

Salma feels her back touch the bottom. Somehow, that lights up all the fire that she saw in Yusra

Mardini's races. She pushes with her feet and turns herself upright, then with all of her strength, she pushes off the tiles, moving her arms the way she saw Yusra swim. Within seconds, Salma breaks the surface. She moves her legs in circles, like Mr. H. taught her earlier, and instead of sinking again, she floats. She grabs her kickboard and removes her goggles. She sees the lifeguard swimming toward her, and Mr. Heatherington stands on the edge of the pool with Riya. They are all staring at her.

"Are you okay?" the lifeguard asks.

"Yeah, I think so." Salma is surprised that she feels totally fine, despite how scared she was a moment ago.

"We thought you were drowning," he says, guiding her to the edge of the pool. Mr. Heatherington holds out a hand to Salma and pulls her out of the water.

"Salma, you are a natural swimmer," he says. "Are you sure this is your first lesson?"

Salma wraps her arms around herself and nods. The teacher smiles and hands her a towel, which she quickly cuddles into.

"I think you have a bright future ahead of you, Salma," he says. "With enough training and determination, you might be the best swimmer this school's ever had."

"No. I will be the best swimmer in the world," Salma announces, to the laughter of everyone around her.

Chapter 4

Salma stands at the edge of the pool and waits for the whistle. She leans forward, her fingers touching her toes, her hair tied up inside her swimming cap. The water will be cold; she knows it. But that doesn't matter. What matters is that she swim as fast as she can.

Salma trains three times a week at school; Mama takes her to the local aquatic center every other evening, too. She spends her days watching swimming videos to better her technique. She is ready for the team tryouts.

Ayman is there, too. He stands a few lanes away in a similar pose. He decided to try out for the team as well. He wears swim shorts and the black goggles his father got him. Ayman looks at Salma, who winks at him before realizing that he can't see the wink under her goggles.

Riya sits in the bleachers. Next to her, Mama holds Nora. The three of them smile widely.

"You got this, Salma!" Riya shouts when she notices Salma looking. She pumps her fist in the air, and Mama cheers next to her.

The whistle is loud and sudden. Salma takes a deep breath and dives into the pool.

Over the past weeks, Salma has mastered the butterfly stroke, just like Yusra Mardini. She moves her arms like a wave to catch and push back water. She tightens her legs together like a dolphin's tail, then dives with her head down like a seahorse. She raises her head for a second, takes a quick breath, and goes under again. *I will be the fastest swimmer,* Salma thinks to herself. *I will win every race.*

Next to her, Salma sees the other swimmers sailing across the pool, bubbles following them. Salma imagines her favorite swimmer next to her, too.

Remember to keep your core strong, Salma, Yusra says to her. Salma squeezes her stomach muscles. *Hold your fingers tight,* Yusra instructs, and Salma presses her fingers together, creating fins. *Breathe smarter, not harder,* the imaginary swimmer whispers. Salma pops her head over the surface, takes in some air, and dips back under.

You are doing great! Yusra says. Salma reaches the end of the lane, flips in the pool, and pushes off the wall with all her might. *You will win this race.*

The water gets heavy. Salma's arms are getting tired. She feels a burning in her chest. Competitive swimming is a hard sport. Sometimes, Salma forgets that with how much she enjoys the water.

The wall at the end of the pool appears blurry through the water. Salma wants to be the first one to reach it. She squeezes all her muscles and pushes one last time. Finally, she touches the wall.

Salma finishes fourth, after Ayman and two other swimmers. She is proud of herself. Even though she didn't win, this is the highest she has ever placed.

She takes off her goggles and looks up, waving at her mother. Mama is distracted. She is talking to three other mothers, all of them wearing the hijab. Salma has seen them in the mosque but rarely speaks to them. They are probably here with their older sons, whose tryouts are right after Salma's age group.

"Great job, everyone," Mr. Heatherington says.

"I did so well today," Ayman announces as they get out of the pool. He finished in first place, as usual. "I don't want to discourage you all, but I'm clearly the best swimmer in this school."

"You're also very humble," Riya says as she joins the group.

"I am actually the most humble person in the world," Ayman insists, and everyone laughs.

As Salma dries off, she looks up toward Mama again. She's pointing at Salma. The women around her look concerned. Mama stands uncomfortably, places Nora on her other shoulder, and walks away. *That's strange. She didn't even wave goodbye.* Salma wonders what they said to her mama. Maybe Salma did something wrong, and that's why Mama was pointing at her?

"I will post the list of those who qualify for the swim team by the end of this week," Mr. Heatherington declares. "Remember, today's race counts, but I'm also considering your performance and improvement throughout the term. Now, off to the showers!"

"Thank you, Mr. H.!" Salma waves at Ayman as he heads to the boys' changeroom. Salma knows she did her best today, but was it good enough to get her on the team? She really hopes so. Her swimming has gotten so much better in such a short time. She knows that given the opportunity, she will soar across the water.

Salma is almost at the showers when she hears someone say her name. She peers behind the lockers and sees a group of older girls changing. They don't notice her. Salma recognizes them from the swim team—she's stayed late after her lessons a few times to watch them practice in the pool.

"Oh, that Syrian girl? What a short little thing!" one of them says.

Another girl laughs. "She doesn't have the right body for swimming. Her legs are so large! She'll never make the team."

"They let anyone try out nowadays," the third insists.

Salma steps back and hides behind the lockers. She feels tears gathering in her eyes. That's not fair. Salma loves her body and thinks it's so amazing that she can move through water the way a bird spreads its wings and flies through the air. It's not fair that these girls are judging her so harshly. They don't even know her.

But . . . what if they are right?

They've been swimmers longer than she has. Maybe

she doesn't have the right body to be part of the swim team. She does look very different from these girls . . . Maybe this means her dream will never come true.

Salma walks into one of the shower stalls and turns on the faucet. She is not sure if it's the water or her tears that wet her cheeks.

Chapter 5

It's a special Friday! The birth of the Prophet is a celebration Salma usually loves: the family goes to the beautiful mosque, with its soft carpets, colorful windows, and intricate mosaic walls. Together, they listen to the lovely hymns, accompanied by the tapping on the daff. Mama got permission for Salma to miss school, so she can join her family.

Salma wants to feel the joy that comes with such

a beautiful day, especially since the celebrations are exactly like the ones they had back in Syria. But instead, she can't stop thinking about those girls in the changeroom.

"Salma, are you okay?" Mama asks on their way to the mosque. Salma has been quiet in the back of the car, which is rare for her. Usually, she plays with Nora who is beside her in her car seat, or chats with Mama and Baba.

"Yeah. I'm just tired from so much swimming," Salma says quietly. She sees Baba checking on her in his mirror.

When they finally reach the mosque, Baba parks and the family separates. Baba is going to go downstairs, where all the men gather. Mama and Salma will climb with Nora to the second floor, where the women and

young children meet. Baba gently pats Nora's cheek, kisses Salma's forehead, and waves at Ayman and his father in the distance.

When Salma, Nora, and Mama get upstairs, Mama hugs her friends, and they exchange pleasantries celebrating the good day. Salma slips away and sits by a window overlooking the floor below, filled with men and young boys. She scoots in behind the window's curtain, hoping no one will try to talk to her.

She spots Baba standing with Ayman and his father. Ayman must be saying something funny, as both men laugh loudly. Ayman flexes his arms, then says something with a big smile on his face. His father looks proud, especially when Ayman waves his arms as if he is swimming. They must be talking about Ayman's progress in his training.

"How could she let her daughter swim in public like that?"

Salma freezes; the woman's voice is coming from the other side of the curtain. The woman can't see Salma but Salma can see her: she is one of the hijabi women who saw her race the other day.

"I know!" another woman says. "Did you see the tiny little swimsuit that girl was wearing?"

"Oh, her mother has no shame," a third woman says. "Muslim women and girls should never wear such clothing."

Salma's blood boils: Why are they talking about her and her mama this way? The Prophet said that gossip is bad, yet they seem to be enjoying it. Why are they judging her for doing what she loves, but not mad at Ayman for doing the exact same thing? Salma feels so angry. She squeezes her fists until her nails leave marks on her palms. She wants to jump out. She wants to scream. Her anger at the girls in the changeroom is now doubled, and she is ready to teach them all a lesson. Salma pushes the curtains aside.

"Salma!" Salma feels a warm hand on her shoulder and turns.

"Granny Donya?"

Granny Donya says hello and her sweet smile brings Salma instant calmness. Her colorful shawl looks warm. She explains that she is back in Vancouver after staying in Victoria with distant relatives for a while. Salma hasn't seen the older woman since they lived together in the Welcome Center a couple of years ago, when Salma and Mama came to Canada. Granny Donya was one of her favorite people there: she helped Salma cook yummy food for Mama and always had Persian desserts to share.

"My good child! I missed you, my little Syrian chef!"

"I missed you, too!" Salma rushes in for an embrace. Granny Donya squeezes her in tightly. They wish each other a happy day. Granny Donya asks Salma for her latest news, and Salma excitedly tells her of all her adventures, including her goal of becoming a great swimmer.

"I think it's a wonderful thing to aspire to, child." Granny's smile is so bright, it lights up the whole mosque.

"I thought so … but there are so many people saying mean things about me, Granny." The anger Salma felt before turns to sadness. "The girls at school say my body is not made for swimming. The women in the mosque say it's not right for me to wear a swimsuit. I feel so much pressure in my heart, when all I want is to be like Yusra Mardini."

"The girls at your school will always find something to yap about, my child." Granny Donya sits on the soft, fluffy carpet and invites Salma to sit next to her. "If it's not your height, it's your weight, or the color of your skin, or the thickness of your hair. There will always be people with time on their hands to speak negatively about you."

"But it hurts when they say these things." Salma burrows into Granny's side.

"You know what happens after a duck dives underwater?" Granny Donya asks. Salma is confused and shakes her head. "The water slides off its back, as if it never were wet. The duck swims, dives, and does what it wants, but it is waterproof, always warm, never inconvenienced."

Salma looks up at Granny.

"Their words are water off a duck's back," Granny Donya says. "They mean very little, while you swim and dive like the beautiful bird you are."

Salma rests her palm in her Granny's hands. She feels the warmth on her fingers. Is Granny Donya right? Should Salma forget about these gossipy people? Salma's anger still feels like fire inside of her. She wants to tell the people saying mean things about her and Mama to stop.

The call for prayer fills the mosque, and Salma and Granny Donya stand to line up with all the other women. Mama looks back with Nora on her shoulder and sees Salma with Granny. She waves at them with a big smile.

"I don't like how these women talked badly about my mama for letting me wear the swimsuit," Salma whispers.

"Do *you* like wearing that swimsuit, Salma?" Granny Donya asks. The question surprises Salma: no one has asked her that before. Salma thinks about how she feels when she puts it on. It's not the best feeling. She wants to swim, so she wants to wear the swimsuit, but she does feel uncomfortable with how exposed her legs and arms are.

"I don't know," Salma says.

"That's a great place to start," Granny replies. "It's time for you to find out."

The voice of the Imam fills the mosque, and everyone quickly raises their palms to their ears, starting the prayer in unison. Salma does the same. She is not sure yet what she wants to do, or how to feel. But being here in this moment, next to her beloved Granny, brings her such comfort.

Chapter 6

Students crowd the school hallway, waiting by the bulletin board. Salma stands in the back with Riya and Ayman, rubbing her palms together nervously. Today, Mr. Heatherington announces who has qualified to join all the different sports teams—including the swim team. Salma wants the chance to swim more races and be just like her hero. But now there's another reason she wants to join the team: to prove those mean girls wrong. She will show them all.

"I am so nervous," Salma tells Riya and Ayman.

"Well, I'm sure I'll qualify." Ayman puffs his chest out and stands taller. "I am, after all, the best swimmer this school has ever seen."

"I don't think Salma is in the mood for your jokes today, Ayman." Riya elbows their friend. Ayman finally glances at Salma and his face drops. He huddles closer to his two best friends.

"I am sure you will make the team, too, Salma." Ayman's voice becomes serious. "I saw you train every day. You gave it everything you had!"

Salma nods. She is thankful for her best friends always being there for her. Even when Ayman is being a bit of a clown, she knows he respects her. He will make a great teammate . . . if Salma makes the team.

"It's just so annoying," Salma finally says. "When you work hard, Ayman, everyone celebrates you. When I work hard, it seems a lot of people have opinions on what I do, or what I wear, or how I look."

Ayman is about to say something, but Mr. Heatherington appears out of the teachers' lounge. He holds a stack of papers. The crowd parts as he walks calmly toward the board and pins the lists to it, taking his time.

"He is taking forever!" Salma says between her teeth.

Finally, Mr. H. walks back to the teachers' lounge. The students rush to read the lists. Shouts of excitement and sighs of disappointment fill the hallway.

"I can't look," Salma says. "I'm too scared."

"Don't worry, Salma, I'll look for us." Ayman merges into the crowd, shouldering students out of his way. Salma feels Riya's hand squeezing hers. After a moment, Ayman reaches the bulletin board. Salma's heart beats so hard, she thinks the whole school must hear it. Finally, Ayman turns around and pushes his way back to Salma and Riya. His face is blank.

"Come on, what does it say?" Riya shouts. "The suspense is too much!"

"Well," Ayman says slowly. "All I can say is that . . ."

Salma's breathing is shallow. Her face feels so warm. If Ayman doesn't share the results right this second, there is a strong possibility she will hit him over the head with her math book.

". . . I qualified for the swim team," Ayman

announces. Both Salma and Riya jump in excitement for their friend.

"And what about Salma?" Riya asks.

Ayman holds his breath. He gets a sad look on his face and stares straight at Salma. "I am so sorry, Salma," he whispers.

Salma's heart falls to the ground. Her dream is about to be crushed. She needs Ayman to say the words.

"But," Ayman finally says, "you also qualified for the team!"

"You little . . . !" Riya shouts, pushing him playfully. He laughs hysterically. "That's not a good joke."

"I think it was a great joke, actually." Ayman is very proud of himself.

Salma takes a deep breath. Her dream is coming true. She made the swim team. This is the best news she's ever heard. Her hard work was worth it. All the tired nights and the difficult techniques. All the challenging exercises and the painfully cold water. It was all worth it.

"Congrats, Salma!" Riya gives Salma a big hug.

"Thank you!" Salma says. "I can't wait to tell Mama and Baba."

"I know they will be very proud of you, Salma. *Everyone* we know is going to be so proud!" Ayman says.

Salma's blood freezes. She suddenly feels heavy. Now more people will see her in her swimsuit. She'll be on the team with those mean older girls, and they will find even worse things to say about her. And what if people keep spreading gossip about her mama in the mosque?

Riya gives Salma a huge hug, bringing Salma back to the joyful moment. These negative thoughts are all water off a duck's back. Today she will celebrate. She is part of the swim team; and the first swim meet, where she will compete against teams from other schools, is only a couple of weeks away.

Chapter 7

After parting ways with Riya on their walk home, Salma daydreams about meeting Yusra Mardini. What would Yusra say to her? Would they have much to talk about? Salma would ask if it was hard for Yusra to adjust to her new life as a refugee, the way Mama and Baba struggled—or even the way Salma struggled. Did she also have to deal with people who did not support her dream? Did she feel uncomfortable in her swimsuit, too? How did she go through this journey and make all of these decisions on her own?

Salma climbs the stairs to her home and slips into the apartment. She can't wait to tell her parents the good news. She spots Mama in the living room, but pauses before Mama sees her. Mama's eyes are red, and her tears fall like a waterfall down her cheeks. *What's going on?*

"Mama, are you okay?" Salma rushes toward her. Mama quickly dries her tears with a tissue. "Is Baba okay? Did something happen to Nora?"

"Oh, it's nothing to worry about, Salma." Mama's voice is a bit broken, as if she has been crying for a while. "Everyone is all right. I just got some onion tears."

Salma can tell that Mama is hiding something.

There are no onions anywhere. She wraps her arms around her mama's waist. "Mama, tell me the truth," Salma says. "What happened?"

Mama leans down, squeezes Salma in, and kisses her on the forehead.

"When did my daughter become the sweetest child in the world?" Mama smiles softly. "You're right that I'm upset, but I promise you it's a grown-up thing. Everything will be okay."

Salma nods, still worried. Mama clears her throat then asks Salma about her day. Remembering her good news, Salma jumps away and stands in the middle of the room. She

proudly announces that she qualified for the swim team.

"That's such wonderful news, Salma! I'm so proud of you," Mama says. "I can't wait to see Baba's reaction. Help me clean up while we wait for him to come home."

When he finally arrives, Baba is also excited for Salma. "I knew all of your training would pay off, Salma," he tells her. "You are a determined girl, and nothing can stand in your way."

Salma feels a bit shy. She holds her hands behind her back and sways as she listens to her father's encouraging words.

The evening passes, and Salma almost forgets about Mama's tears. But as she heads to the living room to say goodnight, Salma can't help but overhear her parents' conversation.

"They are all talking about us at the mosque," Mama whispers. "They are saying we don't know how to raise our daughter."

"Let them say what they want to say." Baba's voice is angry, but reassuring. "They are ignorant and gossipy. Those are not the values of our religion or our culture anyway."

Salma's anger gathers in her throat like a fireball inside of a dragon's mouth. She is so mad that these women made her mama cry. And she is done with overhearing conversations. "They are all wrong!" Salma charges into the living room. Mama gasps.

"Salma! This is not how we raised you. We don't eavesdrop," Baba says.

"I am sorry, Baba," Salma says. "I didn't do it on

purpose. But I heard the women at the mosque gossiping, too. I don't know why they are talking badly about us while celebrating their own sons. Why can't I also have a dream like Yusra Mardini?"

"You shouldn't worry about that, Salma," Mama says. She starts to say more, but instead a single tear escapes from the corner of her eye. Mama slides back on the sofa, and Baba takes her hand, comforting her. He softly touches her cheek. The two of them look at Salma.

"We are raising two wonderful girls who will grow up to be their own women," Baba says. "We are proud of you for following your dreams, Salma. That's all that matters."

Salma doesn't know what to say. She leans in and kisses Mama on the cheek.

"I'm sorry, Mama," Salma says. "I don't want you to feel bad."

"It's not your fault, Salma." Mama takes a deep breath. "Go to bed. Everything is going to be all right."

Salma wishes her parents goodnight, kisses Nora on the forehead, then returns to her bedroom and quietly closes the door. She didn't know her dream was causing such pain for her parents. Why? Why do they care so much about what she wears? Are the women at the mosque right? Should she not be swimming? Should she give up her dream to avoid all of this?

No one talks about Ayman's swimsuit, or what he wears, or why. No one gossips about him or says he shouldn't be a swimmer. Salma doesn't think that's fair at all.

Salma slips into her bed, turns off the light, and

tries to go to sleep. But the thoughts keep gathering in her mind. What should she do? Should she drop the swimming lessons? She still feels uncomfortable with the swimsuit... But is she uncomfortable because *she* doesn't like it, or because she doesn't like the mean things these people say about her?

The gossip hurts; the comments made her cry. Maybe her dream is not worth it anymore. Maybe she should quit altogether.

The clock keeps on ticking, yet Salma cannot fall asleep.

Chapter 8

The pool is very cold today. Salma floats a couple of inches underwater. She tries her best to find the fresh feeling she gets when swimming, but instead all she feels is the heavy pull of the water. She opens her eyes, then closes them again, searching for the calming silence. Instead, she hears the strokes of every hand and leg in the whole swimming pool. She holds her breath as long as she can, then pops up to get some air.

"Salma!" Mr. H. calls from the other side of the pool. "Why are we not doing our best?"

"I'm sorry, Mr. H."

"You are part of this team now, Salma," Mr. H. insists. "We all have to be at our best!"

"Maybe Salma can be the best towel girl on our swim team," Salma hears Ashley say from the deck. She's

one of the girls Salma overheard in the changeroom. Clearly, she isn't going to get any nicer, even though Salma made the team. "She can bring towels to the ones who actually win races."

"That's not a nice thing to say." Mr. H. looks back, and Ashley cowers between her peers.

"Salma!" Ayman shouts. "You are doing great!"

Salma gathers more air in her lungs, then goes back to swimming. She can't bother herself with these girls now. Not when she is in the deep end of the pool. She needs to focus on her training. Their first swim meet is next week, and the team they will face is known for having strong swimmers. She needs to spend every drop of energy she has on this.

Still, Ashley's words hurt her. She feels them echo inside of her head, even underwater.

Salma searches for her muse below the surface. Where is Yusra Mardini when Salma needs her the most? She listens for Yusra's words of encouragement so she can swim faster. But all she hears are the negative words of the women at the mosque and the girls on her team. She shivers, tightens her lips, then pushes herself up to the surface just in time to hear Mr. Heatherington's whistle.

"Training is done for today, folks," the PE teacher says. "Hit the changerooms!"

Salma gets out of the pool and grabs her towel. She left it by the edge to make sure she could wrap herself up the second she got out. She doesn't want anyone to see her in her swimsuit. The older girls rush past Salma in the doorway, and a couple of them turn back to give her a weird look. Salma tightens her towel around her body, then quickens her step. She hurries to shower and get back to her classroom, where she waits for Ms. Singh to return from the lunch break.

"You look tired, Salma," Riya says. "Are you okay?"

Salma sighs and finally tells Riya and Ayman about the mean girls on the swim team and the conversation she overheard at the mosque. Ayman's jaw drops as he listens. Riya shakes her head in disappointment.

"These people are awful, Salma," Ayman says. "I feel bad. Everyone I know loves that I joined the swim team."

"You don't need to feel bad," Salma mumbles. "It's great you are getting this support. I just wish I was treated the same way."

"Is it all because of your swimsuit?" Riya asks. "That seems silly."

"To be honest, Riya . . ." Salma pauses for a moment. "I only wear the swimsuit because I have to. I feel so awkward walking around the pool wearing it."

"Can't you wear something else?" Ayman asks.

"I don't know. I never thought about it." Salma realizes that she never questioned the swimsuit itself. Maybe a different swimsuit would be more comfortable. She should ask about this. Who knows what other types of swimsuits are out there?

"Maybe if you wear something different, all of these people will stop criticizing you!" Ayman adds. Ms. Singh enters the classroom and warmly waves at her students as she sets up her board for the next class.

Is Ayman right? Will she be able to swim in peace if she wears something else? That's very tempting, Salma thinks.

But what would Yusra do? Would she change something about herself for others? No. She would stand up for her own needs.

"If I'm going to change what I wear, I will only do it for myself," Salma insists. She recalls what Granny Donya told her a couple of weeks ago. "The people who want to say mean things will always find something to be angry about. I will not change what I wear for them."

Riya looks at her best friend with awe. "Salma, this is the wisest thing you have ever said."

"I'm proud of you, Salma," Ayman adds.

Salma is proud of herself, too. This new attitude feels not only good but also right.

The school bell rings, and Ms. Singh starts writing on her whiteboard.

Chapter 9

"Salma, we are going to be late to this afternoon's prayers!" Mama calls from the living room, and Salma quickly sneaks out of her parents' bedroom.

"What are you wearing?" Mama asks. Salma has one of her mother's hijabs on her shoulders. Baba got it for Mama in Damascus. It's beautiful, covered in lovely branches and flowers, and Syrian-made. She lets the long shawl slip down her back like a superhero's cape, with a knot tied at her throat.

"I like the colors of this shawl," Salma says. "I want to wear it to the mosque today."

"Like a hijab?" Mama asks. "Do you want me to wrap it around your head?"

Salma isn't sure. She explains to Mama that she wants to wear the shawl but doesn't want to cover all her hair. "It's how I want to wear it today. Is that okay, Mama?"

The knot suddenly gives, and the shawl slips off of Salma's back and down to the floor. Mama smiles. She kneels next to Salma and turns her around to face the large mirror in the hallway. Mama expertly ties it like a cape with a hood, using colorful pins. The green shawl fits Salma's shoulders perfectly. Together, mother and daughter stand facing the mirror, both of

them in their hijab.

"I think it looks beautiful on you," Mama wipes away a proud tear.

"Thank you, Mama."

In the mosque, everyone comments on Salma's beautiful outfit. All the women gather around her and congratulate her on wearing it. Even the women who were gossiping about her mother join the circle. They, too, examine Salma's hijab.

"Are you going to wear the hijab properly one day, Salma?" one of these women asks.

"I will wear the hijab when I want. I think I can be whatever I want to be, and wear whatever I want to wear," Salma announces proudly. "And that includes my swimsuit."

The woman frowns at that answer. She is about to

say something, but a loud laugh interrupts her.

"Look at how beautiful you look today, Salma," Granny Donya says. "The hijab looks great the way it is, too."

Salma rushes over to Granny Donya. The two hug joyfully. "Mama helped me put it on," Salma says. "Don't you think it's beautiful?"

"It looks great on you, Salma," Granny Donya says. "And more importantly, I can tell you *feel* great in it, too."

Mama joins them as the other women walk away. Granny Donya plays with Nora for a second, then blesses her with a Quranic prayer and wishes her a long and healthy life.

"What made you decide to wear the hijab today?" Granny Donya asks. Salma pauses, considering her words.

"I think it's beautiful, and it makes me happy to wear it," Salma says. "Maybe one day I will decide to cover all my hair. But for now, I just wanted to show all these women that my mama raised me right."

"Oh, my little child," Granny Donya is shocked. "I can't believe you'd worry about these gossipy people."

"I am sorry you heard us discuss this, Salma." Mama squeezes Salma closer to her. "This is a conversation for grown-ups. You shouldn't worry about me."

Granny listens calmly then pulls Salma closer. "Have you thought about my question, Salma?" Granny whispers.

Salma nods. "I don't feel good wearing the swimsuit, but I still want to be a swimming champion like Yusra Mardini."

The voice of the Imam comes from downstairs,

calling everyone to prepare for prayer. The women stand and line up next to one another. Granny Donya holds Salma's hand as she stands up, then points to all the women in the mosque.

"Look at all these women's hijabs, Salma," Granny Donya says. "Some cover most of their hair, others cover all of their hair and their neck. Some wear a black or a brown burka that covers them head to toe, while others wear colorful hijabs like you and your mama."

Salma looks at the sea of women around her. The many hijabs in their many colors look so beautiful: like the sparkles of light when water is pouring out of a spring in the sunshine. She smiles as she sees how different everyone's hijab is, yet they are all moving in the same way, preparing for their prayers.

"I hear that there are also many ways you can wear your swimsuit," Granny Donya continues. "There is the diving suit, with short sleeves for the arms and short pants for the legs. There is the burkini, which covers all of your body including your hair. There are many options out there for you."

"Wow!" Salma says. "I've never heard of any of these! How do you know all these things, Granny?"

"I might be old, but I do know how to search the Internet!" Granny Donya laughs. "I just needed my reading glasses and my son's phone."

Salma smiles. Maybe one of these swimsuits could be the perfect fit for her. Maybe she will finally be able to feel totally comfortable at the pool. She is so excited to explore her options.

"You are a good swimmer, Salma." Mama stands on Salma's other side. "We will support you in following your dream."

In that moment, standing between Mama and Granny, Salma feels as if the whole world can challenge her, and still she will win the race. Salma has never felt as powerful and capable as she feels right now.

The prayer starts; Salma raises her hands next to her green hijab and whispers the name of Allah.

Chapter 10

Finally, it's the day of the swim meet. Salma is not afraid; she is not worried. She is ready.

Well, she might be a bit nervous, but she saw an interview with Yusra Mardini the other day where Yusra said that sometimes nerves are good. If you are nervous, Yusra said, that means you care about what you are doing. And Salma really cares about what she is about to do.

She has been training for weeks, watching videos of her favorite Olympian swimmer, practicing her breathing, and reading all the tips and tricks she can find online.

Salma walks into the girls' changeroom. She opens her gym bag and pulls out her pretty swimming cap and her goggles. She doesn't need the snorkel today. She hasn't needed her kickboard in months. She reaches all the way in to her elbow and finally grabs her new swimsuit. It is a diving suit with long sleeves down to Salma's wrists, and short leggings that end close to her knees.

It's black with yellow striping—the same colors Yusra Mardini wore for the Olympics.

She examines the new suit closely. It is exactly what she wants to wear today. It feels perfect in every way. When she put it on in front of Mama a couple of days ago in the sports shop, it felt comfortable and fit her like a glove.

"Did you see that the Syrian girl is competing today?"

Salma hears the voice from the other side of the changeroom. She knows the same girls are talking about her. But this time she doesn't care. She is not here to listen to other people's opinions of her. Their words are water off a duck's back. She is here to be the swimming champion she dreams of being.

Instead of following the conversation, Salma turns

her back and walks into the stall to put on her new swimsuit.

When Salma walks out onto the pool deck, she runs into Ayman. She gasps.

"What are you wearing?" she asks loudly.

His swimsuit is almost identical to hers.

"It's not fair that we compete in the same race, but we are treated differently," Ayman says. "So, I decided to put on the same suit as you."

Ayman does a superhero pose, then a strongman biceps pose. "No one stands a chance now." He raises both of his arms up. "I'm winning this race!"

"Not if I win it myself," Salma teases. She feels supported by her good friend and teammate. She thanks him, then they high-five and walk side by side toward the pool.

Salma walks proudly past all the parents attending the swim meet. She sees Baba and Mama cheering for her. Even Nora, with her tiny little face, has a big, beautiful smile, as if she is cheering for her older sister as well. Next to them stands Granny Donya and Ayman's father. Khalou Dawood is there, too, with his husband Michael, sitting beside Riya's Maa.

Riya appears holding a big towel and a bottle of water. She rushes over to Salma's side.

"You are going to do amazing," she says.

"Thank you so much, Riya." Salma holds her best friend's hand close to her heart. "I know I can always rely on you."

With every step she takes, Salma feels her parents, her friends, and her family beside her, supporting her and showing their love. Even Yusra Mardini, her champion swimmer, proudly walks alongside her.

Salma always thought that her dream was to join the swimming team, and win the race. The truth is: she feels differently today. This is the team she wants by her side. With them, all dreams can be achieved. Salma feels like the sun, surrounded by all the planets and stars in the sky. She is full of energy and ready to win this race.

Salma steps up onto the platform. She winks at Ayman who stands at the other end of the pool. Like always, she knows he can't see the wink under her goggles, but she is sure he winks back. She leans down and touches her toes, waiting for the whistle.

"Good luck, Salma!" Salma hears her mama cheer from the platform. She smiles. Today, she doesn't need luck. She trained hard. She worked harder. She memorized her strokes and learned how to move her body through the water like a wave. Today, she will win this race.

The whistle blows and Salma dives in.

The water welcomes Salma, as if she is a duck diving deep. She rhythmically moves her body. Both arms together, both legs, too. The bubbles escape her nose and crown her swimming cap for a moment, then rush behind her. At first, Salma watches the other swimmers around her, making sure she is ahead of them. But before she even goes up to take her first breath, she forgets about them.

She is now swimming by herself. The pool is her playground, and she knows it well. She feels a smile forming on her face once more. The quiet underwater and soft bluish colors fill her soul with calm. She pushes her arms again and finds herself moving faster, like an elegant sea creature born to swim. The water slides down her new swimsuit. It feels like feathers: waterproof, warm, protective, designed to make her the fastest swimmer there is.

She goes up, takes a quick breath in, and dives back down.

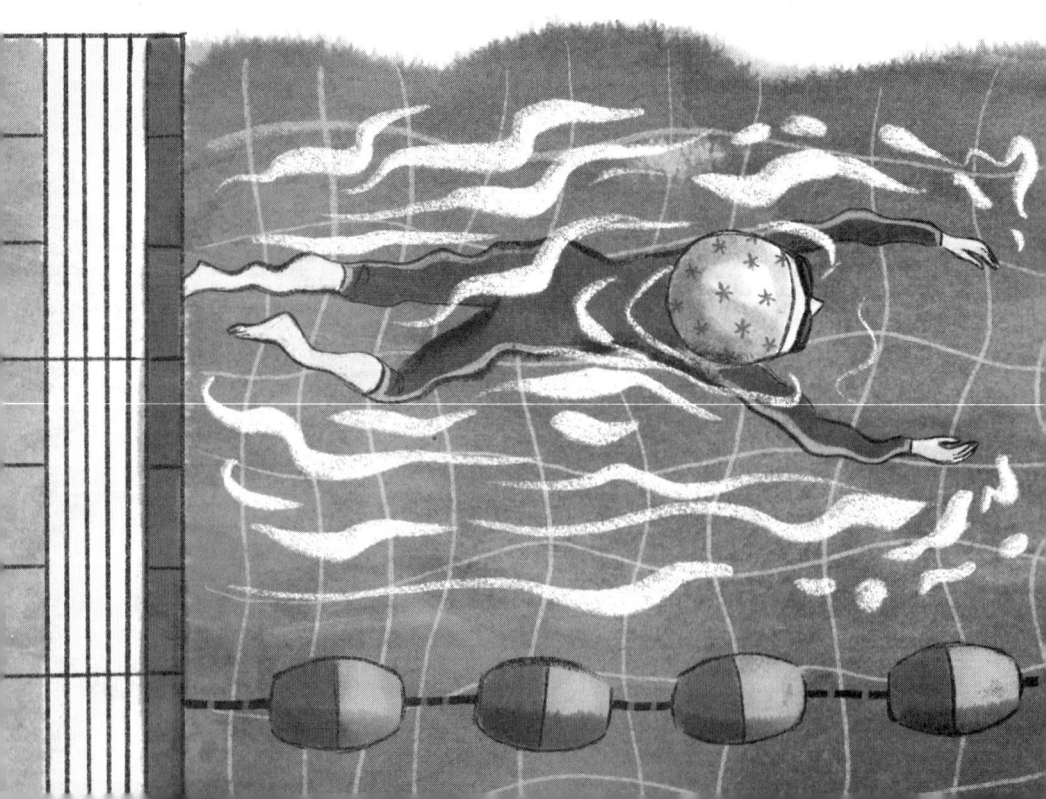

Her goggles fog a bit, but that's okay. She knows which direction to go, and can still see the lines of the pool she is so familiar with. The opposite wall is getting closer, and she quickly flips around, using her momentum to push off the wall, then swims back in the other direction—even faster this time. The goggles

slip up to her forehead, but she doesn't care. Salma can finish this race with her eyes closed.

Another deep breath. For a second, she can hear all the cheers from around the pool, before she dives underwater again.

Salma pushes harder. She moves her body faster. She kicks the water deeper. Now that she can't see, she counts in her head: she knows that she can cross the whole pool is less than two minutes. She's got this. She opens her eyes for a moment and sees the wall approaching. She is almost done. Finally, she slaps her hand on the edge of the pool.

Salma can't see anything. She hears one of her teammates ask who won the race, but it doesn't matter to her anymore. Her eyes are full of water, but she is so joyful. She rubs them, then looks up to see her family and friends all cheering for her. She is full of happy thoughts. This was the dream. She has just swum well, and her loved ones are all there to celebrate with her. This is the moment she wanted to have. She doesn't need to hear Mr. Heatherington announce the results to know she is a winner.

- A hero is someone who inspires you—maybe they did something that you thought was cool or made art you thought was brilliant; maybe they are a good person you know who really means a lot to you.
- A hero is someone who can be a compass for you—leading you by example and helping you navigate your choices and actions.

Salma's hero is the celebrated Olympic swimmer Yusra Mardini because:

- Yusra is a Syrian-born refugee just like Salma. Salma is proud to be a Syrian girl and loves that she has other Syrians to look up to.
- Yusra swam across the sea to help her sister and her family, and then she found her way to a new home. This means a lot to Salma, who also loves her family, especially her new sister Nora.
- Yusra competed in the Olympics, and Salma knows only the strongest, most dedicated people get to go to the Olympics.

Ayman's hero is Iron Man, a fictional character that he loves! Ayman's choice was easy for him because:

- Iron Man has a lot of gadgets: a robot he talks to, a 3D computer he can play video games on, and an iron suit that he can use to fight bad guys. Ayman would be great at fighting bad guys too if he had an iron suit.
- Iron Man is kind. Even when he hides it with jokes, he always finds a way to help others. Ayman likes to prank his friends, but he also cares about them.
- Iron Man is friends with both Black Panther and the Hulk. Ayman wishes he was friends with Black Panther, too. Black Panther wouldn't be friends with Iron Man if Iron Man wasn't a good guy.

Riya's hero is her aunt Arundhati, her Amma's youngest sister and the free spirit of the family. Riya looks up to Arundhati because:

- She is outspoken and knows what's happening in the world around her. Riya hopes to be as smart as her aunt one day.
- She is funny and loves life. She even took a ride on the carousel with Riya in Playland and laughed all the way through. Riya

wants to be this adventurous one day, and to keep laughing and enjoying kids' things.

- She cries watching movies, even the funny ones. She feels for the characters on the screen. Riya wants to be as empathetic as her aunt when she grows up.

Now, it's your turn to come up with your own hero! Circle one of the options. Is your hero:

- a celebrity
- someone you know
- a fictional character

What is the name of your hero?

When was the first time you heard about your hero?

What makes them special to you?

What's the biggest lesson you've learned from your hero so far?

Like Salma, Ayman, and Riya, list three things you love about your hero and why these things matter to you. Fill in the blanks:

My hero is _____. I know this because _____. I also want to be _____like my hero, because _____.

My hero is _____. I know this because _____. I also want to be _____like my hero, because _____.

My hero is _____. I know this because _____. I also want to be _____like my hero, because _____.

About the Author

DANNY RAMADAN made Canada his home in 2014 after leaving his homeland of Syria and becoming a refugee in Lebanon. Since then, Danny has written multiple books for both kids and grown-ups. People seem to think Danny knows how to write well. To his surprise, they keep asking him for more books.

In Vancouver, the place Danny calls home, he met Matthew, the love of his life, and married him. The two adopted the bestest dogs in the world, Freddie and Dolly, who are named after singers from the '80s you are too young to know and who nap exclusively in Danny's lap every afternoon. When Danny is not writing, he is playing video games.

About the Illustrator

© Dana Bron

Just like Salma, **ANNA BRON** moved to Canada with her family when she was very young. She remembers helping her parents with English and making friends in school with kids from all over the world. She always loved to draw from her imagination and when she grew up, she became an illustrator and animator. She gets to work on lots of fun projects, from drawing kids' books to designing unique characters and working on short animated films. Her favorite things to draw are horses, birds, and mountains. When she's not drawing, she loves getting outside to hike and ski.

Moving across the world was Salma's first big adventure. Now you can join her on even more adventures in her new home—from cooking Syrian food, to becoming a big sister, and more!

Also available as e-books!

Salma the Syrian Chef
978-1-77321-374-3 PB
978-1-77321-375-0 HC

All Salma wants is to make Mama smile. A homemade Syrian meal might cheer her up, but Salma doesn't know the recipe, what to call the vegetables in English, or where to find the right spices!

Salma Makes a Home
978-1-77321-762-8 PB
978-1-77321-761-1 HC

Salma's dad is finally joining the family in their new home! But what if Baba misses Syria so much that he decides to go back?

Salma Writes a Book
978-1-77321-803-8 PB
978-1-77321-802-1 HC

When Salma learns her family is growing, she sets out to write a guidebook on being the best sibling ever . . . and finds out that being a big sister is going to be harder than she thought!

Salma Joins the Team
978-1-77321-829-8 PB
978-1-77321-828-1 HC

Salma is determined to be a champion like her hero, the Syrian Olympian Yusra Mardini. But first she needs to learn to swim!

Don't miss Book 4, coming in Winter/Spring 2025!